P9-ELS-617

No Nap for Benjamin Badger

by Nancy White Carlstrom
illustrated by Dennis Nolan

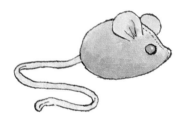

Macmillan Publishing Company   New York

Collier Macmillan Canada   Toronto

Maxwell Macmillan International Publishing Group
New York   Oxford   Singapore   Sydney

Macmillan Publishing Company
866 Third Avenue, New York, NY 10022

Collier Macmillan Canada, Inc.
1200 Eglinton Avenue East, Suite 200
Don Mills, Ontario M3C 3N1
First edition
Printed in USA.

10 9 8 7 6 5 4 3 2 1

The text of this book is set in 18 point Plantin Light.
The illustrations are rendered in pen and ink watercolor.

Library of Congress Cataloging-in-Publication Data
Carlstrom, Nancy White.
No nap for Benjamin Badger / by Nancy White Carlstrom; illustrated
by Dennis Nolan.
       p.   cm.
    Summary: When Ben refuses to nap, Mother Badger tells him
rhymes about all the animals that take naps until they both fall asleep.
ISBN 0-02-717285-6 $13.95
[1. Badgers—Fiction. 2. Naps (Sleep)—Fiction. 3. Sleep—
Fiction. 4. Stories in rhyme.] I. Nolan, Dennis, ill.
II. Title.
PZ8.3.C1948No 1991
[E]—dc20 90-42564

For the Mullers
Marlene and Leo
Anna and Peter
In celebration
of children
and poems
—N.W.C.

For
Erinn
and
Sean
—D.N.

No nap for me, said Benjamin Badger,
Benjamin Badger the Third.

I'm two and a half
He said with a laugh.
Much too old
For taking a nap.
Haven't you heard?
Ben Badger the Third
Who's going to be three
Says, Never,
Not ever!
No! No nap for me!

Now, said Mama Badger,
You surely must know
That all living things
Can't keep on the go.
There's a time to be fast
And a time to be slow.
And whether you like it,
It's so all the same.
Sometimes you must stop
Before starting again.
Let me tell you, my son.
Listen now, my dear Ben.

Butterflies snooze.
After choosing a spot
On the sweet-smelling flowers
Their fluttering stops.
You may think they are planning
Great flights for the night.
They aren't scheming,
They're dreaming
In warm summer light.

Grasshoppers rest
From the heat of the day.
Their hopping has stopped
As they flop to the shade.
Relaxing in hammocks
Of green grassy blades.

The bullfrogs, as well,
Take a break from their song.
Sometimes it is short,
Sometimes it is long.
And when all their croaking
Has finally ceased,
If you listen you'll notice
A time of great peace.

And the spiders who work
At remarkable speed,
After spinning their webs
Sit and swing in the breeze.
And I'm sure their young spiders
Don't run off and hide.
They are happy to nap
And hang on for the ride.

And though not surprising,
It's still very true.
Why, the turtles of course
Always take their naps, too.
They snuggle in mud
That is oozy and cool.
The soft gentle lapping
A nice napping pool.

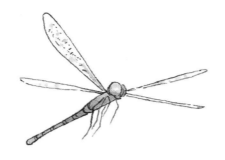

Dragonflies skimmer
The cattails and pond.
Dragonflies shimmer
To sleep with a yawn.
The bugs, how they stretch
And the worms, how they curl.
Believe me, my son,
It's a big napping world.

That's how it has been
And how it should be
For beavers and beetles
In water and tree.
And Benjamin Badger
Who's going to be three.

Wise Mama Badger
Kept whispering rhymes
As Benjamin listened
And finally, in time,
His head touched the pillow
His eyes closed in sleep
Ben Badger was napping
From head to his feet.

Ben's Mama sat back
With a sigh and a smile
Enjoying the stillness
And after awhile
She gazed at her son
In his sound badger doze.
Then she scribbled a poem
As she sniffled a rose.

A good book, a rose,
And a pot of tea
A pen and paper
What could be
Sweeter
Even more sublime?

Ben Badger sleeping
At naptime!

Then tired Mama Badger
Dropped paper and pen
Put her feet on the hassock
And napped with son Ben.